Yankee Doodle

and Other Best-loved Rhymes

Yankee Doodle

and Other Best-loved Rhymes

Capella

This edition published in 2008 by Arcturus Publishing Limited
26/27 Bickels Yard, 151–153 Bermondsey Street,
London SE1 3HA

ISBN: 978-1-84837-136-1

Printed in China

Illustration by Ulkutay & Co Ltd
Compiler: Paige Weber

CONTENTS

This Little Piggy

This little piggy went to market.
This little piggy stayed at home.
This little piggy had roast beef.
This little piggy had none.
This little piggy cried, "Wee, wee, wee!"
All the way home.

Yankee Doodle

Yankee Doodle went to town,
Riding on a pony.
He stuck a feather in his hat
And called it macaroni.

Yankee Doodle, keep it up,
Yankee Doodle Dandy,
Mind the music and the step,
And with the girls be handy.

Father and I went down to camp,
Along with Captain Gooding,
And there we saw the men and boys,
As thick as hasty pudding.

There was Captain Washington,
Upon a slapping stallion,
Giving orders to his men,
I guess there were a million.

Yankee Doodle, keep it up,
Yankee Doodle Dandy,
Mind the music and the step,
And with the girls be handy.

Higgledy, Piggledy

Higgledy, Piggledy, my black hen,
She lays eggs for gentlemen;
Sometimes nine, and sometimes ten.
Higgledy, Piggledy, my black hen!

Twinkle, Twinkle, Little Star

Twinkle, twinkle, little star,
How I wonder what you are.
Up above the world so high,
Like a diamond in the sky.
Twinkle, twinkle, little star,
How I wonder what you are.

When the blazing sun is gone,
When he nothing shines upon,
Then you show your little light,
Twinkle, twinkle, through the night.
Twinkle, twinkle, little star,
How I wonder what you are.

Then the traveler in the dark,
Thanks you for your tiny spark.
He could not see which way to go,
If you did not twinkle so.
Twinkle, twinkle, little star,
How I wonder what you are.

Three Blind Mice

Three blind mice, three blind mice,
See how they run, see how they run!
They all ran after the farmer's wife,
Who cut off their tails with a carving knife.
Did you ever see such a sight in your life,
As three blind mice?

One For Sorrow

One for sorrow,
Two for joy,
Three for a girl,
Four for a boy,
Five for silver,
Six for gold,
Seven for secret,
Never to be told.

Little Tom Tucker

Little Tom Tucker,
Sings for his supper.
What shall he eat?
White bread and butter.

How will he cut it,
Without any knife?
How will he marry,
Without any wife?

There Was a Crooked Man

There was a crooked man,
And he went a crooked mile.
He found a crooked sixpence,
Against a crooked stile.

He bought a crooked cat,
Which caught a crooked mouse,
And they all lived together,
In a crooked little house.

Rock-a-Bye, Baby

Rock-a-bye, baby,
In the tree top.
When the wind blows,
The cradle will rock.

When the bough breaks,
The cradle will fall.
Then down will come baby,
Cradle and all.

Three Young Rats

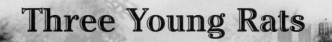

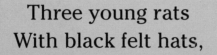

Three young rats
With black felt hats,

Three young ducks
With new straw flats,

Three young dogs
With curling tails,

Three young cats
With demi veils,

Went out to walk
With two young pigs,

In satin vests
And sorrel wigs;

But suddenly
It chanced to rain,

And so they all
Went home again.

Georgie Porgie

Georgie Porgie, pudding and pie,
Kissed the girls and made them cry.
When all the boys came out to play,
Georgie Porgie ran away.